Much Ado About Nothing

Much Ado About Nothing

Retold by **Jenny Oldfield**

Illustrated by Serena Curmi

A & C Black • London

First published 2011 by
A & C Black Publishers Ltd
36 Soho Square, London, W1D 3QY

www.acblack.com

Text copyright © 2011 Jenny Oldfield
Illustrations copyright © 2011 Serena Curmi

The rights of Jenny Oldfield and Serena Curmi to be
identified as author and illustrator of this work respectively
have been asserted by them in accordance with the
Copyrights, Designs and Patents Act 1988.

ISBN 978-1-4081-2402-4

A CIP catalogue for this book is available from the British Library.

This book is produced using paper that is made from wood grown
in managed, sustainable forests. It is natural, renewable and
recyclable. The logging and manufacturing processes conform
to the environmental regulations of the country of origin.

Printed and bound in Great Britain by
J F Print Ltd., Sparkford, Somerset.

Contents

List of characters

Claudia Ricci, *Lite reporter*

Leonato Ianucci, *AC Messina's owner*

Don Pedro, *AC Messina's coach*

Claudio, *AC Messina's star striker*

Benedick, *AC Messina's top defender*

Hero, *Leonato's daughter*

Beatrice, *Leonato's niece*

John, *Don Pedro's brother*

Antonio, *Leonato's brother*

Conrade, *John's friend*

Borachio, *John's friend*

Margaret, *Hero's friend*

Ursula, *Hero's friend*

Luigi Salvo, *AC Messina's physio*

Dogberry, *security guard*

Priest

Act One

We Are the Champions

Major hunk alert! This is your *Lite Entertainment* correspondent speaking to you from the baking tarmac of Messina airport as our cup-winning squad fly home to a heroes' welcome. *Lite* has been given special access to film events on the days following the biggest international footballing triumph since Italy won the World Cup. My name is Claudia Ricci and I'm happy to be your guide.

As you can see, a massive crowd of fans has gathered to greet the all-star team. Amongst them a gaggle of A-listers are here for this celeb-strewn celebration. I honestly can't move for Gucci gowns and Laboutin heels.

Here on my right I can pick out the club's sponsor, international financier Leonato Ianucci, his daughter, Hero, and her girl-about-town cousin, Beatrice, all gagging to congratulate our winning team. And lucky me – I'm near enough to listen to the AC Messina lowdown from long-time team physio, Luigi Salvo, who flew in ahead of the boys.

'They're coming into gate H5, right?' Leonato wants to know.

'Yeah, that's them taxiing towards us as we speak.'

'Terrific final. Great play. But did the game throw up any serious injuries?' Leonato is already looking ahead, worrying about the next match.

'A couple of minor niggles, that's all.' Luigi is happy to put the money man's mind to rest.

'And Claudio was Man of the Match?'

The physio is craning to get a look at the plane, but he can't get away, not from the man who pays his wages. 'He deserved it. He was everywhere – up front to score, back in defence when it was needed. The kid was phenomenal!'

'His family will be over the moon,' Leonato comments.

I lean across with my microphone, recording every word.

And now Beatrice butts in. To be fair, it's been at *least* sixty seconds since the girl last opened her mouth. 'So is Benedick on the plane with the others?' she asks Luigi.

'The last I heard he was.'

'I'm amazed!' (She isn't really – she's just saying it for effect.) 'That he reached the airport in time,' she explains to Hero and her uncle. 'What with all those girls he had to say goodbye to.'

'That's a little harsh,' Leonato warns. He's just noticed me and my cameraman. 'Benedick played brilliantly. He was up there with Claudio for Man of the Match.'

'Oh, Man of the Match. I'm sure that's what the girls called him,' Beatrice flashes back.

Uncle Leo picks up on what she's trying to imply. 'I'm talking about his performance on the *field*, what are *you* talking about?'

Beatrice can't resist playing on the double meaning. 'Yes, Uncle – Benedick's "performance on the field", what else?'

Leonato doesn't bat an eyelid. 'I don't know and I don't *want* to know anything about

Benedick's private life, unless it gets into the papers and affects his game. All I do know is that you two will be at each others' throats before he even has time to unpack his cup-winner's medal.'

Cue more smart remarks from Beatrice. 'The latest score is four–nil, to me. Benedick may be a soccer hero, but off the pitch he doesn't stand a cat in hell's chance, and he knows it. Anyway, Luigi, who's he hanging out with and corrupting these days?'

Luigi looks for wriggle room. He glances at his watch, then out at the runway.

'Come on – give me a name,' Beatrice insists.

'I guess that would be Claudio,' Luigi mumbles apologetically.

'Oh, totally tragic! Poor Claudio!' Beatrice goes OTT as usual. 'Tell him to ditch Benedick at once. Claudio's young and innocent – the paparazzi will grind him to a pulp!'

Luigi is half swamped by a crowd of photographers rushing to gate H5. 'I didn't hear that,' he mutters.

'Take no notice,' Leonato says. 'Beatrice loves to be outrageous, but she doesn't mean anything by it.'

Beatrice looks as if she's about to answer back *again*, but now the plane doors are open and the team are stepping down onto the red carpet. Cameras flash, and at last poor Luigi can escape.

Don Pedro, immaculately dressed in a dark-blue designer suit, is leading the boys into the full glare of the crowd. *Click-flash-click*! He makes a beeline for Leonato and clasps his arms, kissing him on both cheeks. 'Good to see you, sir.'

'I'm overjoyed – wouldn't have missed this homecoming for the world,' Leonato tells him.

There's more camera action, more shoving and yelling.

'Claudio, look over here! Hold up the cup. Look this way!'

Click-flash-click! Claudio raises the silverware

15

above his head, Benedick by his side.

In the hustle and bustle, Don Pedro turns to Hero and does the huggy-kissy thing again. 'You have one proud dad,' he tells her. 'You must be very happy for him.'

'Hero was *born* happy,' Beatrice cuts in. 'When have you ever seen her sad?'

Suddenly, Benedick materialises out of nowhere, ready to suck up to the boss. 'Who wouldn't be happy to have Leonato for a dad?'

And Beatrice is back, quick as a flash. 'Who asked you?' she wants to know.

But Benedick doesn't even look her way, let alone answer the question. 'Still here?' he sighs. 'Unluckily for you. You've never been my flavour of the month, remember?'

'Doesn't bother me.' The guy is A-list arrogant and doesn't care who knows it. 'The whole world is full of women ready to fall at my feet. One exception makes no difference to me. Anyway, I'm not interested in wannabe WAGs.'

'Thank god! That makes one less sex-mad, self-centred womaniser to worry about.' Beatrice doesn't pull her punches. 'And, amazingly, it's the one thing we agree on. Like you, I haven't got time for the opposite sex. I'd donate all my Laboutins to charity, every single pair, rather than show a nano-grain of interest in a run-of-the-mill soccer hero!'

This time, Benedick can't help reacting. He's angry and he shows it. 'Good – keep thinking like that. And mind you keep your claws away from my face!'

'My claws couldn't make you uglier than you already are.'

'Pot – kettle – black!' Benedick retorts, as the press crowd in.

'Typical!' snorts Beatrice. 'And don't worry – I'm not about to lower myself to your level.'

Leonato sees it's time for him to step in and do something quick. And he only goes and invites the whole team to spend a month at his swanky seaside villa. That's *everyone* – players,

17

coaches, physios, plus me and my camera crew. Even Pedro's brother, John, is included, though rumour has it that John and Pedro were involved in some major brotherly spat during the early stages of Messina's cup bid. I hope to find out more about that later.

John growls a quick thank you. I mean, who would say no to sun, sea and as many WAGs as you could possibly want?

Now there's one last smile from the team for the world's press, before the open-top bus whisks everyone away to Leonato's luxury pad.

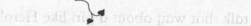

I'm still a fly on the wall, squeezed in behind Claudio and Benedick, as the Man of the Match sneaks a chance to confide in his new best buddy.

'Did you clock Hero back there at the airport?'

'Sure.' Benedick is busy waving to the fans that line the streets.

'Didn't you think she was looking hot?'

'You do realise that you're asking the opinion

of the biggest commitment-phobe on the planet.'
Benedick is still waving.

'I'm serious!' Claudio insists.

'OK, if you must know, I think Hero's too short – I prefer tall girls. And she's dark – I prefer blondes. Apart from that, yeah – she's hot. Though I still don't give her more than seven out of ten.'

'I'm not kidding, Ben. Tell me what you *really* think.'

'Why? Is she on the market?'

Claudio leans forward in his seat. 'You don't talk that way about a girl like Hero!'

At last Benedick stops waving to give the kid the benefit of his wide experience. 'Since you scored the winning goal, you can get any girl you want – and don't look at me like I said something you didn't already know!'

'OK, but I still say Hero's different. Nicer, sweeter, prettier...'

'You're kidding. Are we talking about the same woman? Now take her cousin, Beatrice.

19

If she'd just keep her mouth shut, you'd soon realise she's way above Hero in the looks department. Anyhow, you're not thinking of making a move in Hero's direction, I hope.'

I notice there's a long silence between the question and Claudio's answer.

'I guess that's a yes,' the striker finally admits.

Just then, the bus driver puts on the brakes. We have arrived at Leonato's villa.

'What am I hearing?' Benedick cries. 'And what has happened to my new drinking buddy? You do realise that you're putting your head right into the noose?' He means it. There's a long pause, and then he adds, 'Just don't come running to me when you're bored. Hey, Pedro, listen to this!'

The team coach is about to get off the bus, but he turns to join in Benedick's bit of fun. 'OK, guys, what's up?'

'Promise not to tell anyone,' Benedick grins. 'Only Claudio here is in *lurve*! And before you ask, the lucky girl is Hero!'

'Hold on...' Claudio's protest is pretty feeble. 'OK, I admit it,' he sighs, going all red and awkward. Bless!

The coach gives it some thought. 'Good luck to you, son.' More thought. 'She's a nice girl.'

'You're not just saying that?' Claudio checks.

'No, it's true.'

Benedick breaks the mood by bursting out laughing. 'Absolutely true!' He gets up and heads for the door. 'Just don't ask me for advice – I know nothing about *lurve*!'

'Cynic!' Pedro shouts after him, then slaps Claudio on the back.

They climb down from the bus, and vanish between the marble columns at the entrance to Leonato's villa.

'I reckon Benedick's not as anti-woman as he makes out,' Claudio confides to his coach as they go inside. 'It's all a big act.'

'I heard that!' The man himself stops in his tracks. 'Listen, my mother's a woman, I'll give you that. But that's as far as it goes. I wouldn't trust another not to make a fool out of me, and that's the reason I plan to stay single for the rest of my life.'

'Ha!' Pedro's expression says he's heard it all before. 'What's the betting you fall for some girl and start acting the lovesick fool before we know it?'

But Ben's having none of it. 'I may fall sick for other reasons, boss, but not over a woman!'

'Yeah, yeah...'

'If I'm wrong, you can tell me what an idiot I've been. I'll own up to it, no problem,' he insists.

Pedro winks at Claudio and they join the rest of the players who are crowding round the infinity pool at the back of Leonato's villa. 'Stranger things have happened,' he jokes.

Benedick strolls to the edge of the terrace and looks out over olive groves to the distant hills. 'If I do fall in love and get married, feel free to make me a laughing stock,' he says.

'But I'm telling you straight, I'd rather walk into the epicentre of an earthquake, the eye of a tornado, whatever...'

'I hear you,' Pedro laughs. 'But right now I'm starving. Go and ask Leonato what time we're going to eat.'

Our soccer star doesn't take well to being treated as a gofer, but he knows better than to argue with his coach. So he trots off on the errand while Pedro and Claudio lie down on loungers beside the pool.

It's not long before Claudio is back on his favourite topic. 'Boss, do you mind if I ask you a favour?' he mutters shyly.

'Ask away. You won us the cup – you're my golden boy. Is it to do with the girl?'

'Hero? Yeah. I knew her before, but I never took much notice of her. There was too much on my mind in the build up to the cup. But now that's over, it's hit me hard. I think she's gorgeous. I can't get her out of my head – her hair, her face, her skin...'

'Way too much information!' Pedro raises a hand to stop the flow. 'You want me to have a word with her? I know you're shy, kid, so I take it that's the favour you wanted to ask.'

'Thanks. That's what I was leading up to.'

'Consider it done. I'm happy to help, and here's the plan.' Pedro talks to Claudio as if they're discussing team tactics before a match. 'Leonato's throwing a big party tonight. Fancy dress. So let me dress up as you and treat Hero to some of my best chat-up lines. I'll tell her I'm smitten and all the rest. She'll fall for it, big time. Then I'll sort it all out with her dad. By the time the party's over, you'll be able to call in the wedding planner!'

This might sound to you like a halfway decent plan, given that Claudio's mega shy and all that, but I have the knack of making sure I'm in the right place at the right time and I soon hit a complication. It happens a few minutes later, when Leonato is fussing about music for the party and he bumps into his doddery older brother, Antonio.

'Do you have a minute?' Antonio asks.

'I can give you thirty seconds,' Leonato agrees.

'I was out by the pool just now. I overheard Pedro talking to Claudio.'

(Oh dear! Careless talk can be dangerous. You especially, Pedro, should know how important it is to check for the presence of reporters...)

'So?' Leo counts the seconds.

'Pedro's been telling Claudio he has a thing about ... well, actually that he's *in love* with your daughter! He plans to tell her tonight and then ask you if he can marry her.'

(And if you're gonna snoop, Antonio, then at least follow the basic rule of all good journalism and that is to get your facts right!)

'OK. You'd better warn Hero what to expect.' Leonato dashes off.

In my opinion, even though he's rushed off his feet, the guy should have given this news about his daughter a lot more thought.

I'm still working out the implications of this basic factual error and putting finishing touches to my fancy-dress costume when I run into laugh-a-minute John and a shady-looking guy called Conrade, who I haven't seen before.

'Why the long face?' Conrade asks. And he makes a small attempt to cheer up John.

But misery guts is having none of it. 'Why fake it?' he grumbles. 'I am what I am and I intend to stay miserable – OK!'

Conrade doesn't see it that way. 'Not OK. I'm all for faking, especially if you want to stick around and get back in Pedro's good books.'

If John wants to carry on lounging by the pool, this seems like good advice, but here's what Mr Sunshine thinks:

'I'd rather be kicked out onto the street than act all nicey nicey. I was born bad and that's the bottom line, take it or leave it. Nobody puts a muzzle on me, and people had better watch out, because I bite!'

I'm shaking in my shoes, but Conrade comes over with the pop psychology. 'Maybe you could channel all this anger instead,' he suggests.

But then another piece of lowlife called Borachio turns up. (You'd think Leonato would have more sense than to let these guys into his house.) 'The party's started,' he announces. 'And expect a major splash for the gossip mags – a marriage is on the cards.'

(Tut-tut, the world and his wife seems to have got hold of the story, but at least Borachio has the right end of the stick.)

'Claudio wants to propose to Hero,' he tells John and Conrade. 'But it's complicated – the kid's too shy to do the deed, so Pedro's planning to go in disguise and chat up Hero for him.'

When he hears this, John's miserable face lights up. I'm talking personality transplant. 'I can use this!' he cries. 'And when I'm through with Claudio, he definitely won't be my brother's Man of the Match!'

Act Two

Party With the Stars

Hello again, viewers, as you join me, Claudia Ricci, to party with top footballers and fashionistas in the idyllic Italian Riviera. Tonight I can reveal exclusively for *Lite Entertainment* the full facts about the stars and their stunning fancy-dress costumes. And you can bet it's going to be a gathering that the guests will remember for the rest of their lives!

Right now I'm standing here on the sprawling terrace of Leonato's fairytale villa, where no expense has been spared on an extravagant display of white peonies and roses, mingling with thousands of Swarovski crystals and glimmering candles. Let's step back and watch as our AC Messina heroes gather under the stars.

Look, here comes Leonato, checking off the guests.

'Has anyone seen John?' he asks.

Antonio tells him no, then Beatrice comes in with one of her famous one-liners: 'The guy's so sour it gives me indigestion just looking at him!'

This leads into a heated debate between her, Hero and Leonato about party pooper, John. Bea compares him with Benedick, and can't resist putting them both down.

Leonato tuts. 'You'll never find a husband if you keep on like that.'

'Fine by me,' Beatrice retorts. 'Lord save me from a husband with a beard for a start. It'd be like sleeping with a woolly blanket!'

'So find one without a beard,' Leonato suggests.

'What, you mean a lady-boy!'

This brings gasps and giggles, so Bea carries on. 'At least a man with a beard is a genuine grown-up. No, I don't want either one with a beard or one without. I'd rather show up as I am in hell and get sent to heaven for being a virgin. I'd find lots of eligible guys in heaven and I'd be perfectly happy!'

It's obvious Antonio doesn't get Beatrice's sense of humour. He drops Hero a line of what he thinks is sensible advice: 'Don't try to be like her – do what your father tells you.'

'Yeah, Hero, do your duty,' Beatrice grins. 'But don't say yes to an ugly guy on any account!' And she laughs out loud when old Antonio says he hopes she'll find herself a husband one day. 'Never!' she cries.

Leonato gives up on her and turns to his daughter. 'Remember, if Pedro proposes to you tonight, your answer is yes.'

'Wait, wait!' Beatrice steps in. 'Don't let Pedro push you into anything rash. Men do that, you know. They sweep you off your feet during the wooing phase, like they're involved in some up-tempo dance routine – you haven't got time to work out what's real and what's fake. Then it all slows down for the wedding march, and after you're married, love goes pear-shaped and completely out of tune.'

'Too true,' Leonato can be heard to mutter. He's probably lost a fortune in divorce settlements.

A boy band starts to play and now it's

dressing-up time. We all put on our masks and a new group of guests burst onto the terrace. Before they disappear behind their disguises, I pick out Pedro, Claudio, Benedick, John and his buddy Borachio, plus a load of other hangers-on. Pedro makes a beeline for Hero.

Lights, camera, action!

'Come for a walk,' is Pedro's opening line.

Pushover Hero says yes. They go out past the pool, where it's quieter.

But more interesting for me and my crew right now is what's occurring between Beatrice and Benedick.

'So, should I know you?' she asks from behind her mask. Obviously she already recognises him.

'No. Should I know *you*?' He's put on a funny false voice that makes me want to laugh.

Beatrice lets him have it with both barrels. 'Did you hear the latest? Motor-mouth Benedick is going around telling people *I'm* too up myself! D'you know Benedick? He's the joker who hangs out with Pedro and Claudio, telling lousy gags. No one likes him – they all talk about him behind his back.'

Benedick is so upset, he almost drops the act. Luckily for him, the band cranks up the volume and the pair of them get dragged onto the dance floor, leaving John and Borachio plenty of time to get their knives into unsuspecting Claudio.

'*Benedick* – over here!' they hiss, knowing full well who he really is.

Claudio's confused, but he decides to play along with their so-called gaffe.

'Did you know my brother fancies Hero?' John says. 'You know her, don't you, *Benedick*? Couldn't you have a word – tell her Pedro's out of her league?'

'How do you know Pedro fancies her?' Claudio stammers.

'I just heard him chatting her up.'

'Me, too,' Borachio chips in, before the slimy pair drift off.

This leaves Claudio not thinking straight and ready to believe anything. He's so discombobulated, he starts talking to himself: 'Pedro lied to me. He's chasing Hero for himself, the rat. That's what happens between mates when there's a woman in the picture. Anyway, I'd better kiss goodbye to any chance I had of getting her.'

Watch out, Claudio, here comes Mr Commitment-phobe, Benedick himself. Now *he's* not going to be any help, is he?

'Sorry, mate, you have to face it – Pedro made a play for Hero and she fell for it.' Like Beatrice, Benedick never holds back.

'Good luck to him,' Claudio mutters.

'Who'd have thought it?'

'Look, Benedick – just leave me alone, OK.'

'Hey, don't shoot the messenger,' Benedick raises his hands, but Claudio has had enough and storms off, leaving Benedick to talk to himself – the habit must be catching!

'Wow! Beatrice didn't even recognise me

back there beneath my disguise. She said I'm the saddo with the naff sense of humour, who hangs out with the team coach. Is that really what people think? Nah – that's just sourpuss Bea. Well, I'll soon get my own back!'

Cue more music, with me lurking among the flowers and Pedro strolling on the terrace without a care in the world.

'Hey, Ben, have you seen Claudio anywhere?' the coach wants to know.

'Yep. He was just here, looking down in the mouth, and I can understand why.'

Pedro is puzzled. 'What's up?'

'You two are like a couple of kids climbing trees looking for a bird's nest. Then he finds one and you snatch it from him – *that's* what's up.'

'Don't worry, it only looks that way – just wait and see.' Pedro thinks he has everything under control, as always. 'Anyway, I hear you and Beatrice have had another tiff.'

Stand back – now Benedick's about to go off on one!

'You could say that. Listen, she's been bad-mouthing me, calling me names, stabbing away at my reputation. I tell you what, boss, I wouldn't marry her if she was the last woman on earth. Anyway, can we stop talking about her, please? She's trouble with a capital T.'

Pedro grins, spins Benedick around and points him towards a girl in a glittery angel dress complete with halo and wings (the costume has to be ironic, surely!). 'Not so fast – here she comes!' he hisses.

Benedick panics. 'Don't you have a job for me to do?' he pleads with Pedro. 'Anything. I'd rather get sent on a mission to Mars than have to talk to her!'

'Stay here,' Pedro insists.

'No, I can't stand this!' Boss's orders or not, Benedick is out of there.

Pedro watches him shoot off, then turns to Beatrice all serious. 'That's it – I'm afraid you've lost Benedick,' he says, taking her to one side.

'I did have him once,' Beatrice admits.

(Am I hearing right? Is Bea telling it like it really is for a change? I'll play this back later and think about it.)

'Yeah, I gave him my heart and he broke it,' she adds.

'Try not to be so harsh,' coach Pedro advises.

Beatrice breaks away and drags Claudio, Leonato and Hero across to join them.

'Hey, why so serious?' Pedro asks Claudio. 'Are you sick?'

Claudio grunts one-word answers, like a kid sulking in front of a teacher.

So Pedro puts him out of his misery and delivers the good news. 'I did what I said I would – I proposed to Hero for you and got her dad to agree to the marriage, too.'

'That's true – he did,' Leonato agrees.

It's taking Claudio a while to catch up. He's standing there open-mouthed.

'Say something!' Beatrice urges.

Claudio shakes his head. 'Words fail me!'

So Beatrice turns to Hero. '*You* say something then. Or kiss him!'

That's it – the lovers kiss and we get it on camera. Ah! I can see an exclusive wedding-pics issue of *Lite* magazine coming up!

'One more bites the dust,' Beatrice sighs. 'I'll soon be the only singleton left!'

Pedro laughs at this. 'Want me to find you a man?' he offers.

Beatrice flutters her eyelashes. 'Not unless you've got a brother I don't know about,' she quips.

'No, but will I do?'

(Is he serious? Now *this* could be gossip gold!)

Beatrice, bless her, doesn't let the offer cloud her judgment. 'I'll have you for Sundays,' she laughs. 'But I'd need another for everyday wear.' She pauses, wondering if she's gone too far. 'Sorry, am I pushing my luck here?'

The coach isn't the least upset. 'Don't worry – you're fine. Actually, I like your sense of humour – it's refreshing.'

'Anyway, I've got a job to do for my uncle,' she says and dashes off.

I really like that girl,' Pedro admits to Leonato. 'She's always good for a laugh, even though she won't give closet space to a husband.' He thinks for a bit. 'What about her and Benedick?'

Leonato shakes his head. 'They'd drive each other mad.'

So Pedro leaves it for a bit and asks Claudio about his plans.

I make a quick note – the Claudio-Hero wedding is a week from now. Then I hear Pedro back on the Beatrice-Benedick gig.

'Here's a way of keeping our minds occupied before the big event,' he tells the others. 'How about we take up the challenge of bringing those two together?'

And everyone falls in with the boss's scheme, naturally.

'Excellent.' Pedro plans ahead. 'And Benedick does have *some* good qualities, you know.

He could make a decent husband. So let's get him to the altar whether he likes it or not!'

Fast forward to the next day. The event managers have taken away the flowers and dismantled the marquees. And here come slimy John and that nasty Borachio, noting that things haven't exactly gone their way.

'So Claudio got the girl after all,' John moans.

'Not if I have anything to do with it,' Borachio promises.

'Well, I hate Claudio's guts, so anything you can do to wreck his happiness will be good news to me.'

John hates his brother *and* he hates Claudio. Don't ask me why. The hairs at the back of my neck stand on end, and I'm guessing this is the beginning of something really nasty.

'I know a girl called Margaret,' Borachio explains. 'I can arrange for her to come to the window of Hero's bedroom. Your part is to tell your brother he made a mistake when he agreed to help Claudio propose, because it turns out that Hero's a slapper.'

John frowns. 'Where's the proof?'

'I'll make up something, don't worry. And this will throw a spanner in everyone's works – Pedro's, Claudio's, Hero's. Plus, it'll probably be the death of old Leonato.'

An evil light comes on in John's brain. 'So give me the details,' he whispers.

Borachio obliges. 'OK. Tell Pedro and Claudio that Hero is having an affair with me, and you feel so bad knowing about it that you have to spill the beans. Then bring them to Hero's window the night before the wedding and show them proof. They'll hear me call Margaret "Hero" and she'll say, "Borachio, my love – blah blah!" That should do it...'

The plan goes down a treat with John, and he promises Borachio a big bonus. The two men go slinking off into the shadows like cats that got the cream. And now I'm scouting around by the pool looking for my next big scoop – could it be coming in the shape of Benedick, the love cynic? He's muttering to himself again:

'It's weird how a kid like Claudio can be such a Jack-the-lad one minute and falling head over heels the next. I don't get it. A few days ago it was all free kicks, penalties and the offside rule. Now it's romantic music and sleepless nights spent wondering what to wear for his wedding. Once upon a time, he spoke in plain English, now it's all flowery stuff. Well, I tell you it'll never happen to me. I mean, I've met loads of girls – gorgeous ones, clever ones, even nice ones. And I'm nowhere near falling in love with any of them. She'd have to be all three rolled into one for it to happen, plus she'd be mega rich, classy, talented, never answer back, and I don't care if she's a blonde or brunette! Watch out, here come Leonato, Pedro and the lovesick kid!'

Benedick takes cover behind a trellis, where he reckons he can't be seen. Wrong! Pedro winks at Claudio, while he works out how to use Leonato's sound system. Soon he's playing a track from a World's Best Love Songs CD.

Benedick's pulling puking faces behind the screen, then he gets ready to listen in on the guy talk.

Pedro kicks off in a loud stage whisper. 'So, Leonato, are you absolutely sure that *Beatrice is in love with Benedick*?'

Claudio pretends to be amazed. 'Wow, you're kidding!'

'It's true!' Leonato insists. 'Even though she makes a big show of hating his guts...'

Benedick almost knocks over the trellis in shock. 'Is it possible?' he whimpers.

'Actually she's crazy for him,' Leonato goes on, and here's what happens next:

PEDRO: Are you sure she's serious?

LEONATO: Absolutely – it's the real thing.

BENEDICK (muttering to himself): I'd have sworn this was a set-up, if Leonato wasn't here.

PEDRO: And has Beatrice told Benedick

that *she loves him*?

LEONATO: No, and she swears she never will.

CLAUDIO: Because she's always treated him like dirt in the past.

LEONATO: So she starts to write him a text message, telling him how she feels. Then she deletes it and starts again. I've heard it all from Hero. She says Beatrice thinks Benedick will only laugh if she sends it.

CLAUDIO: Then she cries and tears her hair, whispering his name – 'Sweet Benedick'!

PEDRO: Maybe we should tell him.

CLAUDIO: And let him mock her? Then she'd be even worse off, poor girl.

LEONATO: I feel sorry for her.

PEDRO: Ben's a lucky guy. I think we should tell him.

CLAUDIO: Hero's scared Beatrice might kill herself if it all flies back in her face.

PEDRO: But Ben wouldn't be nasty, would he? Behind that tough-guy front I know there's a soft centre – he can even be witty and charming when he's in the mood. So shall we tell him?

CLAUDIO: No!

LEONATO: Yes!

PEDRO: Let's think about it some more.

And these ham-actors walk off, giggling like schoolgirls, planning their next move. I'm going to leave them to it – let's keep the camera on Benedick and see how he reacts.

'This can't be a con!' he mutters. He's in shock. You can hear his brain booting up like a slow computer and I'm hoping he's not so dazed that he walks straight into the pool. 'They said everything with straight faces, and apparently it all came from Hero. They seemed sorry for Beatrice... Well, if she loves me, I guess I'd better love her back! I know I sometimes come across as being arrogant, so I'm not surprised Beatrice won't admit how she feels. Getting married was never on my agenda ... but Beatrice is a babe. So, that's it – from now on, I'm gonna be madly in love with her, even if the guys do laugh at me. Sure, I said I would stay single, but that's before I decided to tie the knot. Uh oh, here she comes now, and yeah, I think she's definitely got the hots for me!'

(Wrong again, Benedick.)

Beatrice flounces up. 'I've been sent to tell you dinner's ready,' she says.

'Thanks, babe,' he simpers.

(*Babe*? Are you kidding!)

'There's nothing to thank me for. I wouldn't have come if I'd found it a pain.'

'So, it was a *pleasure*?'

'Yeah, like having a knife at my throat. Listen, if you're not hungry, just forget it.' And she stalks off, leaving him to work it out.

'"I've been sent to tell you dinner's ready",' he echoes. 'There's a double meaning in that! "I wouldn't have come if I'd found it a pain", which means she *wanted* to bring me the message. Well, I'm a lowlife if I don't respond. Yes, I'll definitely love her back!'

Act Three

Hotting Up or Cooling Down?

L ove meters at the ready, everyone! You're in for the biggest gossip-fest of the decade, and the question is, can Ben escape his playboy past and will wild-child Bea settle down with her man? 31% of viewers have called in to vote Yes, 69% said No. It's Claudia Ricci, still here at the villa, with my finger on the pulse, and I promise you, thing are really hotting up.

Move number one – Hero tells her friend Margaret the plan:

'Bring Beatrice out here onto the terrace and say that we're talking about her. Persuade her to hide behind that stack of sun loungers so she can listen in on our conversation.'

'Got it!' Margaret dashes off.

Move number two – Hero brings her other girlfriend, Ursula, up to speed:

'We're gonna wait until Bea's in position, then we play Cupid. We're gonna gossip about Benedick – you must big him up, I'll say he's crazy for Bea.'

They see Beatrice sneak in and take up her

place behind the sun loungers.

'Ready?' Hero whispers. Then she turns up the volume.

HERO: No, I'm telling you – *Beatrice is a tough cookie*. No man stands a chance of taming her.'

URSULA (proving she's a quick learner): But you're sure *Benedick's in love with her*?

HERO: I heard it from Claudio and Pedro. They think I should tell her, but I said it was a bad idea.

URSULA: How come?

HERO: It's obvious. *Beatrice is too big headed to listen*. She'll never fall in love with anyone except herself.

URSULA: You're right. Better not tell her in case she laughs in Ben's face.

HERO: There's not a guy on this planet that Bea would fancy, no matter how smart, classy or gorgeous he is. If he's too handsome, she makes her sarcastic lady-boy put-downs. Too dark, too tall, too short – she'll always find something to make fun of. Either the guy talks too little or not enough – he can't win.

URSULA (sighing): That's not good.

HERO: But who's going to tell Bea she's out of order. No, don't look at me – she'd make mincemeat out of me.

URSULA: Why not risk it and tell her anyway?

HERO: No, I've got a better idea. I'll find Benedick and persuade him to forget all about her. I'll invent a nasty rumour to ruin her reputation.

URSULA: Oh, that's mean! But surely Bea's clever enough to see Benedick's good points. In fact, to tell you the truth, Hero, and don't take offence – I rate Benedick higher than your husband-to-be! Talking of which, can I get a sneak preview of your wedding dress?

HERO: It's in my closet. Come and see.

Job done. The girls have sprung the trap and go off arm in arm. Beatrice creeps out in total shock.

'My ears are burning. It can't be true! Am I really that conceited? Well, that's all about to change. And, Benedick, carry on loving me and I'll love you back! I'm even ready to go shopping for a ring, because the fact is, if they say you deserve me, I'm totally ready to believe it!'

As you can see, things are moving fast. I'm roaming the villa with my *Lite* crew, picking up the next scrap of scandal when we come across Pedro chatting with Benedick, Claudio and Leonato in the hot tub.

'As soon as you've tied the knot, I have to leave,' Pedro tells Claudio. 'I've got a meeting in Aragon with the head of the Italian football league. Ben, do you wanna come along to keep me company? You're still fancy-free, I take it?'

'Er, not totally,' Benedick mumbles.

Pedro gives him a long, meaningful look. 'Hmm, now I think about it, you do look a bit more serious than usual.'

'Maybe he's in lurve!' Claudio crows. Nudge nudge, wink wink!

'Never!' Pedro gasps. 'He's lost money on the horses, that's all.'

'I've got toothache.' Benedick gives the worst excuse ever.

The others carry on ribbing him something rotten.

'Yeah, go ahead and laugh,' Ben says. 'It's different when you're the one in pain.'

Claudio is like a dog at a bone. 'Definitely in lurve!' he laughs.

Pedro sets off another chain of quick-fire banter. 'He doesn't *look* like a man in love.'

'Yeah, he does. He's begun to care about the way he dresses for a start.'

'Has he restyled his hair?'

'He's had a shave!'

'That does make him look younger,' Leonato cuts in.

Pedro nods. 'And he's wearing aftershave. You can smell it a mile off.'

'Oh well, that's all the proof you need. You're right, he's *definitely* in love.'

'Plus, he's gone all moody on us.'

Claudio grins and gives Benedick a shove. 'So, who's the lucky lady?'

'It's got to be someone who doesn't know him and his moods,' Pedro says.

Benedick can't take any more. He gets out of the hot tub, wraps a towel round his waist and asks Leonato to follow him into the house.

'Did you hear that, Leonato?' Pedro chuckles. 'I'd bet a lot of money that your niece, Beatrice, is in the frame here!'

Leonato nods and smiles as he goes after Ben.

It's all turning out well for the lads until John turns up to spoil their fun. The atmosphere always changes when this creep is around, like a shadow coming over the sun.

He says he needs a quick word with Pedro and Claudio. 'About your wedding,' he explains to our soccer hero.

Claudio doesn't seem bothered. He tells John to fire away.

Deep breath from the creep, then he begins. 'I know you don't think of me as a mate, Claudio, and I know you've used my brother to help set things up between you and Hero, but I'm here to tell you that the girl is both a cheat and a liar!'

'Who, Hero?' Claudio whispers.

'Yes, Hero!' John's stare is intense. 'It's worse than you think, and if you meet me tonight under her bedroom window, I'll prove it. Remember, this is the night before your wedding. If you still love her after what I have to show you, then go ahead and marry her. But personally, I'd advise against it.'

'Can it be true?' the gullible kid asks.

Pedro says it's impossible.

'Just let me show you!' John urges.

'OK, and if it's true, I'll shame her in front of everyone in the church,' Claudio decides a tad hastily.

Pedro backs him up. He's also a bit hot-headed, you have to admit.

John's happy. 'Don't say a word until tonight,' he warns. This new plan is working well for him and he allows himself a bitter, twisted smile.

It's dark now – the time for John's cunning little plan – and things are really, really hotting up. The booze is flowing freely when Leonato's security team shows up for tomorrow's big event. As ever, we keep our cameras rolling.

The security guys are losers beyond belief. There's a fat dummy called Dogberry in charge. He mangles his words and is as thick as two short planks! And the others don't have a brain cell between them, either.

Dogberry stations a couple of bouncers here in the front courtyard and takes the others round the back of the villa. It's not long before Borachio and Conrade roll through the main door dead drunk. It turns out the alcohol has loosened Borachio's tongue. He's boasting about his big bonus and gives Conrade the lowdown on how he managed to talk Margaret into impersonating Hero so that he could con Claudio into believing he's got engaged to a underhand, dirty love-cheat.

'It's a good job it was pitch black,' Borachio laughs. 'The trick worked perfectly. Now the kid is all set to get his revenge tomorrow!'

But the security guards have heard everything. They step out from the shadows and not so much pounce, as drown the villains in an avalanche of angry words. It's an arrest like you'd never believe.

Next morning and we're up with the lark. Your roving *Lite* reporter has gained exclusive access to the bride-to-be, who has developed bad pre-wedding jitters. Margaret is struggling to do Hero's hair and get her into her dress when Beatrice turns up. The bride's cousin isn't exactly entering into the spirit of things, either.

'What's wrong?' Hero asks.

'I'm not feeling very well,' Bea sighs.

'Maybe you could ask Benedick to give you some medicine!' Margaret sniggers.

Bea turns on her. 'What do you mean, "medicine"?' she demands.

'Nothing!' says Margaret. 'I'm not implying you're in love with him or anything like that. We all know that would be too incredible for words. All I'm saying is he was just like you once, and look how he's changed.'

The conversation is suddenly cut short by Ursula dashing in to tell them that Pedro and Benedick are waiting to take Hero to the church. There's a frantic rush to zip Hero into her dress and run the straighteners through her hair one final time.

Let's move to the terrace, where Leonato is trying, and failing, to grasp what Dogberry is rambling on about.

'Can't you see I'm busy?' he snaps. 'Get to the point.'

'Sir, we've misapprehended two villains,' Dogberry explains. 'Now we need you to cross-quiz them.'

'Question them yourselves,' Leonato says as the limo turns up. 'I've got to get to my daughter's wedding!'

'Yes, sir.' Dogberry is happy to oblige. 'We'll begin the cross-quizzification right away!'

Act Four

Cup Winners' Wedding Fiasco

This is it – the most talked about wedding in years! It's today that AC Messina's star striker is tying the knot, and the lucky girl is due to arrive in church any time now. Our fashion reporter has had a sneak preview and tells us that the bride's necklace (old and belonging to her grandmother) is diamonds, her dress (new) is by Vera Wang, the shoes (borrowed from Beatrice) are Laboutin and the stone in her spectacular ring is a sparkling sapphire (blue).

Claudio and Hero's best boy band 'Urban Crew' play the couple's favourite tune as the wedding party arrives. Big-name guests include team coach Don Pedro and his brother John. Club owner Leonato Ianucci leads his beautiful daughter down the aisle. They stand beside a nervous groom and his best man, the jewel in Messina's defence line-up, Benedick. Hero's cousin, Beatrice, does the honours as chief bridesmaid.

Leonato reaches the flower-decked altar. He hands Hero over to her groom and orders the priest to begin. It's all going very well so far.

'Claudio, have you come here to marry this woman?' the priest asks.

'No,' Claudio says.

Somebody in the congregation coughs and shuffles.

'To *be married to* her.' Leonato puts the priest straight.

The priest turns to Hero. 'Have you come here to be married to this man?'

'I have,' Hero says.

'If any here present know of any just impediment why these two may not be joined together, speak now or forever hold your peace,' the priest goes on.

Claudio turns to Hero. 'Do you know any?'

'None,' she replies.

'And do *you* know any?' the priest asks the groom.

Leonato jumps in. 'I dare answer for him – "None".'

At which, Claudio explodes. 'What men dare

do! What men may do! What men do every day without knowing what they do!'

At first, Benedick is stunned like everyone else, then he tries to laugh it off.

Claudio ignores him and challenges Leonato. 'So, you give her to me freely?'

The old man says, yes, he does. His own hand is shaking as he places Hero's hand in Claudio's.

Claudio flings it back at him. 'Have her! She's rotten fruit that only looks fresh on the outside. OK, so she's colouring up, but don't be fooled – Hero's no virgin bride! I'm telling you, she's already slept with a man – all that blushing proves she's guilty!'

The church is in uproar! Guests are out of their seats, spilling into the aisle. They push and shove, reaching for their mobile phones. Through it all my camera crew keep filming.

Zoom in on Leonato – totally confused.

Move to Claudio – boiling with anger. 'She slept with a man and it wasn't me! Oh yes, she had me fooled – I worshipped her. But it turns out that she's a real slapper!'

Zoom to Hero – almost fainting in shock. 'No, you couldn't be more wrong!' she whispers.

But Pedro backs Claudio and says he regrets the part he played in getting them to the altar, since it's plain to everyone that Hero is a cheat.

We're all speechless. Benedick groans that this isn't looking much like a wedding. He tries to hold Claudio back, but the kid has totally lost it.

'OK, here's the big test,' he tells Hero. 'I have one question and you have to give me a straight answer.'

Hero manages to stammer that she's done nothing wrong.

'So answer me this. Who was the man you were talking to outside your *bedroom* window just after midnight last night?'

Hero answers without a pause. 'I didn't talk with any man last night.'

'This proves your guilt,' Pedro mutters.

He tells Leonato that he, John and Claudio hid in the courtyard and saw it with their own eyes. 'The guy, Borachio, confessed. He says they've had thousands of secret trysts.'

Creepy John comes in with his fifty-cents worth: 'What Hero has done is too terrible even to describe!'

And Claudio sets the seal on things. 'If you were only half as beautiful on the inside as you are on the outside, our life would have been perfect,' he tells Hero. 'But I'm walking away from a cheat and a liar. I'm turning my back on love!'

Hero gasps, puts both hands to her cheeks, turns to her dad for help, then faints clean away. Beatrice kneels down beside her. John grabs Pedro and Claudio and drags them out of the church. End of fairytale wedding. Start of huge headlines – Bride of the Year Ditched at the Altar!

Benedick kneels down beside Beatrice. 'How is she?'

'I think she's dead!' Beatrice cries.

Leonato is out of his mind with shock. 'Better dead than live a life of shame.'

Beatrice tries to revive her cousin. 'Hero, wake up!' she pleads

'No!' Leonato shoves everyone away. 'The humiliation is too much to bear. Hero, you couldn't even deny it. Don't live, don't wake up, because if you do, I'll kill you myself for shame. I used to regret that I only had one child. Now I see you were one too many! I should have adopted a baby off the street so that I could disown it at a time like this. But you were mine and I loved you and praised you, was proud of you, put you above all else. And now you've fallen, you're so soiled and dirty that you can never be clean and pure again!'

This ranting reaction from the old man is not pretty and Benedick is doing his best to calm him down.

'This is a lie!' Beatrice says, jumping to her feet.

Benedick takes her by the hand. 'How do you know? Were you with Hero last night?'

'No.' Beatrice can't give her cousin an alibi and this sets Leonato off again.

'See, she's guilty! John and Pedro wouldn't lie. Claudio wouldn't lie. It broke his heart to stand here and tell everyone. Stay away from her – let her die!'

Seeing that Hero is starting to open her eyes, the priest steps in and takes control. 'Listen – I watched Hero carefully through all of this and I believe she's innocent. In fact, I'd stake my life and reputation on it. Hero, what's the name of the man you were allegedly with?'

The bride's come round enough to whisper her answer. 'Ask Claudio. I have no idea. I swear on my life that I never slept with a man, and if my father can prove me wrong, *then* he can disown me and wish me dead!'

'So the men were mistaken,' the priest says firmly.

Amongst all the confusion, Benedick has

started to get his head around some basic facts. 'I haven't known Pedro and Claudio that long, but we're AC Messina, we're like blood brothers, and I know they would never plan anything this nasty without believing it was true. Which leaves John firmly in the frame as the villain of the piece.'

'If I find he's behind this, I'll get my revenge if it's the last thing I do!' Leonato swings from one extreme to the other.

Then the priest comes in again with a plan. 'Claudio and the others left here believing Hero was dead. Let them carry on thinking that. Everyone can go into mourning, you arrange a funeral, and so on. Soon, they'll start to feel sorry she's dead. That's what happens – we start to miss the things we've lost. So Claudio will remember how happy he was with Hero and he'll regret making this accusation, even if he still thinks it's true. It won't be long until the scandal has faded from people's minds and even though we may never prove Hero's innocence, the public will forget the bad bits and remember the good. After that, Hero will be able to live quietly out of the public eye without any danger that the gossip columnists and scandalmongers will come knocking on her door.'

Whoa, they're talking about me! I'm listening to this attack on the press, the cameras are still rolling and privately I'm not thinking too much of the priest's stupid plan. But who would listen to me, a mere reporter working for *Lite Entertainment*?

For some reason, Benedick backs the priest. 'I promise not to spill the beans to Pedro and Claudio,' he says.

And that's it – they carry off Hero to a secret hiding place, leaving Benedick and Beatrice alone in the church.

'Are you crying?' he asks gently.

'Yes, I can't help it.'

'I'm convinced someone has it in for Hero.' Benedick seems genuinely upset and concerned.

Beatrice takes a deep breath. 'You wouldn't

believe how grateful I'd be to the person who could prove that.'

Benedick waits a while. He leans forward and almost kisses Beatrice, but stops himself just in time. 'I love you more than anything in the world. Isn't that weird?'

Now it's her turn to lean in towards him. 'As weird as the way I feel about you, Ben. I could swear I love you, but I can't admit it and I can't deny it. All I *know* is that I feel sorry for Hero!'

'I swear you love me and I love you!'

Beatrice holds her breath. 'I do – I love you with all my heart!'

They stare into each others' eyes and the world stands still.

'I'd do anything for you,' he whispers.

'Kill Claudio!'

'Never!'

'Then you don't really love me, so goodbye. Let me go!' And with that she runs down the aisle.

'Beatrice!' Benedick runs after her and grabs her by the arm.

'Look what Claudio's done!' she cries. 'He's wrecked my cousin's life. He's shamed her in front of everyone. I tell you – if *I* were a man, I'd kill him!'

'Beatrice!'

'What kind of a guy does what Claudio did? Why don't I have a friend who's man enough to stand up to him? Guys these days are soft and shallow. They say things they don't mean. Let me go away into a corner and cry!'

Benedick holds onto her. 'Stay. I swear I do love you.'

'Prove it,' demands Beatrice. She doesn't back down an inch.

'You honestly think Claudio is to blame?'

'From the bottom of my heart.'

'And I believe you. I'll confront him, kill him if need be. Think of me and what you've asked me to do when I leave, Beatrice. Now go and help Hero.'

He finally lets her go and stands in the church doorway staring up at the sky. He's sworn he'll kill his beloved team-mate as she wanted. How did it come to this, he might well ask.

Now listen up – Bruno, one of our production team, has just come from the villa with news of what's happening with Conrade and Borachio. The security guards arrested them for being drunk and disorderly, remember? Anyway, Bruno says that the fat ass, Dogberry, cross-examined them and eventually found out that John *paid* Borachio to frame Hero and fool Claudio into believing she was cheating on him. Well, we know how that worked out here in the church. When John heard the news about Hero being dead, he jumped in his car and drove straight out of town.

That's proof of the power of rumours, in case anyone ever doubted it. Someone will say something is true and it doesn't even have to be on TV or posted on YouTube for everyone to believe it.

Act Five
Dirty Tricks Exposé

78

It was the high-speed romance to end all romances, between a soccer ace and the glam heiress to a multi-million dollar fortune, derailed by a dirty-tricks merchant motivated by spite. You couldn't make it up!

But now the public displays of affection between Claudio and Hero have turned sour. Cancel the wedding reception, and bring in the relationship counsellors to sort out the biggest romantic train wreck in living memory. And do it before Benedick finds himself in even deeper trouble!

We're back at the villa and Antonio is dishing out unasked-for advice.

'The stress will kill you if you go on like this,' he tells his brother.

'How can you know how I'm feeling unless you've been through it yourself?' Leonato groans. 'Show me the father that doted on his daughter and had that daughter betray his love. If he can stay calm, then I might listen to his advice. But there's no such man. People only counsel patience until they're faced with the same experience themselves, then feelings take hold and push them over the edge.'

Antonio tells him not to be childish.

Leonato says he's only human. 'Even high-minded philosophers complain when they get toothache.'

'So try to turn this rage against Claudio,' Antonio advises, and Leonato jumps at the opportunity the moment Pedro and Claudio show up.

They try to brush Leonato aside, pretending they're in a hurry, which is not a good move under the circumstances.

'You're a cheat!' Leonato yells at Claudio, who looks ready for an argument. 'And I'm not scared of you. I'm telling you face to face that you wronged my innocent daughter and I'm challenging you to a fight, in spite of my age. I'll say it again – you lied about Hero and the shame of it killed her. You are to blame!'

'Me?' Claudio stammers.

'Yes, you!'

'You're wrong,' Pedro says.

'Let me prove it,' the old man begs.

Claudio tries to leave again. Leonato won't let him and soon Antonio is in on the act.

'Come on then, boy!' he taunts, jabbing his finger at Claudio's chest. 'God knows, I loved my niece, and you slandered her and killed her. Boys, arrogant apes, bigheads, ruffians, cowards!' He doesn't stop ranting, not even for Leonato to chip in. 'No, I've got their measure. They're nothing but brash, lying, law-breaking, nasty yobs mouthing off about how tough they are!'

Pedro eventually puts a stop to it. 'I'm truly sorry about what's happened to Hero,' he tells Leonato. 'But I swear that Claudio was telling the truth.' He refuses to hear any more protests and turns his back on the elderly brothers, who storm off.

Pedro and Claudio are laughing about it when Benedick comes in.

81

'We nearly had our noses bitten off by two toothless old men!' Claudio cries.

(He's not exactly Mr Sensitive on this occasion.)

For once, Benedick doesn't see the funny side. 'Actually I was looking for you two,' he tells them.

'Likewise,' Claudio says. 'We hoped you'd cheer us up.' Then he pesters Ben with some lame puns.

Benedick is not in the mood for that. He's so riled, he pulls Claudio to one side. 'You're a villain. Yes, I'm serious! And I challenge you to a fight. You've killed a sweet girl and now it's payback time.'

Claudio still thinks he's messing around, and Pedro doesn't get it, either. He starts teasing Ben about Beatrice, how she said that whenever he opened his mouth he was fake, but even so, she admitted she was smitten.

'When will you bite the bullet and marry her?' the two shallow idiots want to know.

Right now, my opinion of them has slid to an all-time low.

'I'm out of here,' Benedick mutters. 'I'll leave you two to your feeble sense of humour. Pedro, we've been good mates, but no more. By the way, have you heard John's vanished? Between the three of you, an innocent girl has been killed. As for you, kid – get ready for a fight.'

Before Claudio can reply, Benedick dashes off, leaving them dumbfounded and blaming Beatrice for his weird behaviour.

(Question: When is it ever Pedro and Claudio's fault? Answer: Never.)

Now along comes Leonato's tip-top security team with Conrade and Borachio in handcuffs. Dogberry is 'in charge'. He says they've 'misapprehended' the pair for dishonesty, but he has to say it in half a dozen different ways.

'The law is an ass,' he says.

And if you ask me, Dogberry's the living proof!

'What exactly are you accusing them of?' Pedro asks. He realises he won't get a sensible answer out of Dogberry, so he turns to Borachio, who comes over all guilty and confessional.

'I tricked you,' he admits. 'And these lame-brain security guards found out.' He goes on to explain John's con trick involving him and Margaret and then he breaks down. 'Hero died because of our false accusation!' he cries. 'And I'm ready to take my punishment.'

The truth has made Pedro's blood run cold. Claudio says it's like drinking poison. They double-check that it really was John's idea.

Claudio does one of his extreme U-turns. He raises his eyes heavenwards. 'Hero, now I see you as you really were – the girl I truly loved!'

It's time for Leonato to stumble back in, having been told the latest development by one of the security team. 'Which one of you is the villain?' he yells at Conrade and Borachio. Then he turns his sarcasm on Claudio and Pedro. 'Who killed Hero with his lies? You two, plus John. Good on you – I hope you're feeling proud!'

Claudio hangs his head. 'Do whatever you like, but believe me – I was genuinely mistaken.'

'Likewise,' Pedro says. 'And I'm ready to take my medicine, too.'

Leonato is determined to squeeze every drop of blood out of the situation. 'I can't bring Hero back to life, but I want you to put out a press release saying she was innocent. And I want you to write an epitaph for her grave. Then come to my house tomorrow morning. You may never be my son-in-law, Claudio, but instead I order you to marry a girl who is almost Hero's double – one of my nieces. If you do this, I'll be satisfied.'

'I'll do whatever you want,' Claudio sobs.

While Dogberry and his goons haul Borachio and Conrade off to jail, Leonato makes Claudio promise to go through with the new plan.

Surprise, surprise, viewers – there's going to be a wedding after all!

Back on the terrace with the stunning sea

view, we find Ben ordering Margaret to fetch Beatrice. She runs off with the message and meanwhile he tries his hand at penning a love song. It's clear from the start that he's no Elton John.

Luckily for us, Bea arrives to find out the latest news on Claudio.

'We've exchanged insults,' Benedick reports.

'If that's all you've done, I'm leaving,' says the girl for whom the term 'high maintenance' was invented.

'No – stay. I threw down a challenge and am waiting to hear his reaction.' Benedick smiles and tries to lighten the mood. 'Now, tell me, Bea – for which of my *bad* parts did you fall in love with me?'

'All of them!' she says. 'For which of my *good* parts did you fall in love with me?'

They joke a bit more, trying to take their minds off the problem in hand. 'At least life with you will never be boring,' he tells her. Then he asks how Hero is.

'She's not doing well, and neither am I,' Beatrice admits. You do get these glimpses of truth from her sometimes.

'Let my love make you better,' he whispers, moving in for a cuddle.

But the sweet talk is cut short by a message from Ursula.

'The whole place is in chaos,' she tells them. 'It's been proved that Hero is innocent and that John tricked Pedro and Claudio into believing her crime. Come quickly!'

The sun has sunk over the horizon, it's the dead of night, I'm here all alone with my hand-held camera and Pedro and Claudio have come to Hero's grave carrying candles. Claudio reads a poem praising Hero, then there's music and a song, all very sad and solemn.

'Blow out the candles,' Pedro orders. 'It's almost dawn. Time to go to the villa for your wedding to Leonato's niece.'

Daylight and everyone's here at the villa – Leonato, Antonio, Benedick, Beatrice, Margaret, Ursula, the priest and Hero.

Antonio says out loud what everyone's thinking: 'I'm glad it's all turned out OK.'

(In other words, it's been much ado about nothing. So, viewers, stop taking things so seriously, sit back and relax.)

The girls go off into an inner room while Leonato finalises the plans. Benedick reckons this is the moment to seize his chance.

'You realise that Beatrice and I are in love?' he asks Leonato. 'So how would it be if she and I got married today?'

'Fine,' Leonato agrees – a spur of the moment decision, just like that.

Benedick puts in his request in the nick of time, because now Pedro and Claudio are knocking at the door.

Then it's all hustle and bustle to get the girls back in the room, their faces hidden behind veils. Leonato quickly lines Claudio up in front of the priest, alongside Hero-in-a-veil. 'Are you ready to marry my niece?' he checks.

'I'm ready!' Claudio vows. He takes the girl's hand, clears his throat and makes his announcement. 'I swear in front of the priest, I'll be your husband, if you'll have me.'

Hero doesn't keep him in suspense. She lifts her veil. 'When I lived, I was your other wife,' she says. 'And you were my other husband!'

Ta da! Claudio and Pedro go into one of their speechless spasms. Leonato is rushing everyone off to church when Benedick steps forward to steal the show.

'Where's Beatrice?' he demands.

She lifts her veil. 'Here I am.'

BENEDICK: Do you love me?

BEATRICE: No more than reason.

BENEDICK: Then you fooled Claudio and Pedro. They swore you did.

BEATRICE: Do *you* love *me*?

BENEDICK: No more than reason.

BEATRICE: Then you fooled Hero. She

swore you did.

BENEDICK (obviously enjoying every moment of this): They swore you were sick with love!

BEATRICE: She swore *you* were almost dead with love!

BENEDICK: Not true. So you don't love me?

BEATRICE: No. Only as a friend.

It's time for Leonato to break it up. 'Oh, Beatrice, I'm sure you *do* love him.'

'And he loves her,' Claudio insists, fishing a piece of paper out of his pocket. 'Look, he wrote a poem to prove it.'

'And here's one from her to him.' Hero produces another scrap of paper.

Benedick sees that it's game over. 'Magic – here's proof in our very own handwriting! OK, Beatrice, I will have you – but only out of pity!'

'And I'll say yes, too,' she mutters. 'But only after lots of persuasion and to save your life.'

'Quiet!' Ben murmurs, and he kisses her on

the lips. Silence at last, and it's golden.

Ah! The image will get a million hits when we put it on the net.

'So, Benedick, how does it feel to be a married man?' Pedro asks.

'I'm on top of the world!' Benedick grins from ear to ear. 'I don't care what people think. We're all the same – we say one thing, then do another, and that's a fact.' Then he tells Claudio that he's not planning to fight him to the death after all, skimming over the news that John has been arrested and brought back to Messina. 'We'll think about that tomorrow. And you, Pedro,' he says with a wink, 'you need to find yourself a wife!'

Cue music and dancing. There's no designer dress this time, and very few A-list guests, but *Lite Entertainment* still captures the partying on camera. This is Claudia Ricci signing off, with the news that we got our big fat wedding exclusive after all.

About the Author

Jenny Oldfield was born in Yorkshire and now lives there again after a spell in the Midlands, where she read English at Birmingham University.

First published at the age of 24, she has had her *Home Farm Twins* series adapted for BBC television, and has written more than 100 books for adults and children. Her work, including *Horses of Half Moon Ranch*, is available in the UK and America, plus translations into many European languages.

While seeking to update *Much Ado About Nothing*, Jenny tuned into World Cup fever in the run-up to the 2010 event in South Africa. The glamour and gossip surrounding international footballers and their wives and girlfriends seemed exactly right for Shakespeare's fluffy, frivolous rom-com.

William Shakespeare's

AS YOU LIKE IT

Retold by Jenny Oldfield

SHAKESPEARE TODAY

WILLIAM SHAKESPEARE'S

ROMEO & JULIET

RETOLD BY MICHAEL COX

SHAKESPEARE TODAY

WILLIAM
SHAKESPEARE'S

A Midsummer Night's Dream

RETOLD BY

ROBERT
SWINDELLS

WILLIAM SHAKESPEARE'S

The Tempest

RETOLD BY
FRANZESKA G. EWART